Disney's MULAN

Adapted by Katherine Poindexter
Drawings by José Cardona
Painted by Don Williams

A GOLDEN BOOK • NEW YORK
Golden Books Publishing Company, Inc., New York, New York 10106

 Library of Congress Catalog Card Number: 97-77257 ISBN: 0-307-13184-X
A MCMXCVIII

Many, many years ago, in the land called China, there lived a young woman named Fa Mulan. Mulan tried to be like all the other girls and bring honor to her family. But she was not always delicate or graceful.

When Mulan went to see the Matchmaker, she accidentally poured tea all over the woman who was to find her a husband. "You will never bring your family honor!" the Matchmaker snapped.

Mulan returned home. She loved her parents very much, and she couldn't bear to disappoint them.

But her father only smiled. "What beautiful blossoms we have this year," he said, gesturing toward a tree. "But look—one is late." He gently replaced Mulan's comb in her hair. "I'll bet that when it blooms, it will be the most beautiful of all."

Suddenly the sound of horses' hooves pounded through the streets!

"The Huns have invaded China!" the Emperor's aide shouted. "By order of the Emperor, one man from every family must serve in the Imperial Army!" When he called the Fa family, Mulan's father stepped forward.

"No, Father!" Mulan cried. Her father was no longer young and had already bravely served the Emperor in an earlier war.

That night Mulan sneaked into her parents' room. She took her father's notice to report to the army. In its place she left the beautiful comb she had worn in her hair. Then she hurried from the room.

With her father's sword, Mulan cut her long, dark hair. Then she slipped into her father's armor. She would pretend to be a young man and fight in her father's place.

Mulan knew the danger. It was against Chinese law for a woman to be a soldier. What if anyone found out? But Mulan loved her father too much to let him go to war.

In the family temple, the spirits of the Fa Family Ancestors awakened. "That Mulan!" one groaned. "What a troublemaker! If they discover she is a girl, she will bring shame to her family."

The First Ancestor addressed the tiny dragon Mushu. "We must send the most powerful Guardian of all to bring her home," he ordered.

"Okay, okay—I'll go!" Mushu said proudly.

The Ancestors laughed. "You are not worthy," the First Ancestor said with a sneer. "Awaken the Great Stone Dragon!"

The Great Stone Dragon's statue stood outside in the garden. When Mushu tried to wake up the mighty Guardian by banging on his ear, the Great Stone Dragon crumbled into a pile of rocks. Mushu knew he was in big trouble!

Quickly he decided to find Mulan on his own. He would do more than just bring her home, he decided—he'd make her a hero! He had wanted to regain his position as Guardian in the Fa family temple, anyhow. Maybe this would help him do it!

Mushu caught up with Mulan. He let a cute little cricket named Cri-Kee come, too. Crickets were known to bring good luck, and Mulan certainly needed that!

"This is it!" Mushu whispered to Mulan as they neared the soldiers' camp. "Show 'em your man's walk!"

Mulan did her best to act like a man. But when her new captain, Li Shang, asked her name, she was stumped. "My name? It's a boy's name, sir. It's, uh, Ping," she replied.

Mulan trained long and hard with the other recruits. The most challenging task of all was to retrieve an arrow from the top of a tall pole. Not a single recruit was able to do it! But Mulan figured out how to use strength and discipline to accomplish the task.

Once they had finished training, Mulan and the other soldiers marched off into the mountains to face the Huns, who were led by the evil Shan-Yu. In a snowy pass, the Huns launched a surprise attack, showering Shang's army with flaming arrows and then charging down toward Shang's troops.

"Aim the last cannon at Shan-Yu!" Shang cried. Mulan knew she had to think quickly. She grabbed the last cannon and ran toward the attacking Huns. Then she lit the cannon's fuse.

KA-BOOM! The rocket flew into the snowy mountainside, causing an avalanche of snow to bury the evil Huns.

As the avalanche continued, Mulan looked for Shang. At last she found him partially buried in the snow. With a great heave, she pulled him onto her horse and carried him to safety.

"Let's hear it for Ping!" one of the soldiers shouted. "The bravest of us all!"

Suddenly Mulan moaned and held her side in pain. "Ping is wounded! Get help!" Shang cried. After tending to Mulan, the doctor stepped out of the medical tent and whispered to Shang.

Shang stepped back in shock. Ping was really a woman!

Under Chinese law, the penalty for such a grave lie was death!

Shang was hurt and angry at Mulan's deceit. But she had saved his life, so in return he spared hers. Then he and his army rode off for the Imperial City, leaving Mulan behind.

"I never should have come," Mulan said to Mushu. Sadly she gathered her belongings and prepared to head home.

Suddenly Mulan saw that a handful of Huns had survived the battle—including the evil Shan-Yu. They were heading for the Imperial City, where the Emperor lived. Mulan knew that she had to do something!

Mulan raced to the Imperial City, where she found Shang and his soldiers. "The Huns are alive!" she cried. "And they're here!"

"Why should I believe you?" Shang replied coldly as he rode past her. Frantically Mulan tried to warn others in the crowd. But no one listened.

All too soon Mulan's warning came true. Shan-Yu captured the Emperor and held him prisoner in the palace. Shang and his soldiers couldn't get inside. But Mulan had an idea! She dressed three of the soldiers as women, complete with wigs, makeup, and paper fans. The Huns were watching for soldiers, so no one paid much attention when these "young ladies" appeared in a palace hallway.

As Shang fought with Shan-Yu, Mulan and her friends used a line of banners to help the Emperor escape.

Shan-Yu knocked Shang unconscious. Then, furious, he began chasing Mulan. As she ran, Mulan glanced out a window and spotted the tower where all the Emperor's fireworks were stored. With one look from Mulan, Mushu figured out how he could help.

Mulan led Shan-Yu on a wild chase throughout the palace and onto the roof, where she bravely faced him. Just then Mushu arrived—with a rocket on his back! Cri-Kee lit the fuse, and Mushu jumped off just as the rocket scooped up Shan-Yu and carried him straight to the fireworks tower. Kaboom! The rocket hit the tower, and a thundering explosion ripped through the night sky.

As smoke from the explosion drifted away, the Emperor appeared. To Mulan's surprise, he bowed to her. Everyone in the palace followed the Emperor's example. "You have saved us all," the Emperor said. Then he gave Mulan two gifts: Shan-Yu's sword and a pendant bearing the Emperor's royal crest. Finally he asked her to become a member of his council. But Mulan declined the offer. It was time to return to her family.

When Mulan arrived home, she presented the Emperor's gifts to her father. Fa Zhou accepted them with pride, but quickly set them aside and gathered Mulan in his arms. "The greatest gift and honor," he said with a smile, "is having *you* for a daughter." Mulan's heart was filled with love for her family.

Moments later Shang arrived. He had come to find Mulan.

"Would you like to stay for dinner?" Mulan asked with a smile.

Shang smiled back and nodded. At the same time, over in the ancestral temple, the First Ancestor was giving Mushu an approving look. "Oh, all right!" he said. "You can be a Guardian again."

"Yippee!" Mushu shouted . How lucky he and Cri-Kee were to know someone as wonderful as Mulan!